The Real Tilly Beany

The Real Tilly Beany

Annie Dalton
Illustrated by Kate Sheppard

EGMONT

*With grateful thanks to
Azha Kumari Chauhan Field
who created Titch the Witch,
and might be Windstar,
and my daughter Anna
who thought of Cindertilly*

EGMONT
We bring stories to life

First published in Great Britain in 1991
by Methuen Children's Books Ltd

This edition published in 2004
by Egmont Books Ltd
239 Kensington High Street
London W8 6SA

Text copyright © 1991 Annie Dalton
Illustration copyright © 2004 Kate Sheppard

The moral rights of the author and the illustrator have been asserted

ISBN 1 4052 0056 1

5 7 9 10 8 6

Typeset by Dorchester Typesetting Limited and
Avon DataSet Ltd, Bidford on Avon
Printed and bound in Great Britain
by the CPI Group

Contents

Rainbows Inside   1

No Tilly at All?   8

Buffalo Stew   18

Oats and Beans and Barley Grow   37

Witchworks   43

Matilda Seaflower   60

The Jellybear's Picnic   86

Cindertilly   106

Abracadabra!   133

Rainbows Everywhere   152

Rainbows Inside

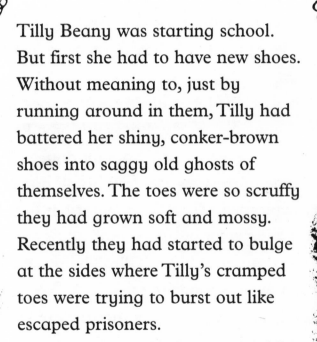

Tilly Beany was starting school.
But first she had to have new shoes.
Without meaning to, just by
running around in them, Tilly had
battered her shiny, conker-brown
shoes into saggy old ghosts of
themselves. The toes were so scruffy
they had grown soft and mossy.
Recently they had started to bulge
at the sides where Tilly's cramped
toes were trying to burst out like
escaped prisoners.

'Oh dear,' said Mum. 'I hadn't
realised how much you'd grown,
Tilly.' They were on the bus, going
into town.

Tilly knew her mum was worrying the shoeshop lady would tell her off for being a bad mother. With four children to bring up, Tilly's mum didn't always remember about new shoes.

'Tell her it only just happened this minute,' said Tilly helpfully. 'And as soon as she looks at them I'll suck my toes in as far as I can.'

Then as the bus sailed past the park she said, 'I have grown big, haven't I, now I'm five? Why can't I go to school all day?'

'None of the new children go all day at first,' explained Mum. 'You might get too tired. Doing a lot of new things all at once can be tiring, you know, Tilly. They want you to have a chance to settle in.'

Tilly scowled, swinging her mossy, bulgy shoes against the seat. She thought doing new things was wonderful. It was doing the same *old* things that was so tiring. Every time she went to boring old playgroup and had to sing 'The Wheels on the Bus' and 'Five Fat Sausages' all over again, she yawned and yawned until she turned nearly inside out.

'I'm perfectly settled into school already,' said Tilly, in a grumbling voice. 'I've seen the gerbils and the stick insects. I've seen my peg with the red umbrella picture where I've got to hang my coat and my shoe-bag. I've met my teacher and she read us that story about the goose that was really a swan. Anyway I know all about school from Tom and Sophie and Kate. I know *everything* already.'

Tilly's brother and sisters were older than Tilly so they always got to do everything first. It was no fun, always being last in the game of growing up. Sometimes Tilly did feel it was like some puzzling game of hopscotch. As soon as she landed on the same square: Hurray! Here I am, now I'm as grown up as you are – *Hop*! They had

gone leaping ahead of her to the next part
of the game and poor Tilly was left behind
again. Sometimes she was afraid she
would never catch up.

Tilly knew she
was every bit as big and
sensible as Tom and her sisters. Sometimes
she was sensibler than Sophie, who had
started giggling in a really silly way lately
whenever boys talked to her.

And Tilly was much *much* sensibler than
Tom, who had once turned on the gas under
a pan of baked beans, forgotten all about it

and gone off to watch telly while the pan bubbled, burned and steadily turned as black as soot, all by itself in the kitchen.

And who was it who smelled the smell? Who was it who ran in right away and turned off the gas and yelled for Mum because the saucepan was much much too hot for children to touch? Sophie Beany? Kate Beany? Tom? Huh? Not on your life! It was *Tilly* Beany, that was who. Sensible, amazingly grown-up Tilly Beany.

But when other people looked at Tilly all they seemed to see was her ordinary *outside*; a small round five-year-old person with round green eyes and dark-brown, shiny kind of hair, and two round bashed-up-looking knees.

And that wasn't who Tilly really was at all *inside*! She might have the same boring hair and face every morning when she woke up and looked at herself in the mirror, but she was never the same *inside* from one day to the next. From minute to minute even. Inside she was always changing, like clouds that could rain or thunder or turn themselves into rainbows. Inside she was as big as a whole world full of different people, young and old and in-between; running, laughing, quarrelling, turning cartwheels. Why couldn't everybody else see that? Even her mum and dad couldn't see it, and they loved Tilly very much.

Suddenly, Tilly felt scared as if she might somehow have turned invisible without noticing it. As if nobody could *really* see her at all. As if she was some sort of ghost. She grabbed at her mum's hand in a panic. But her mum smiled back at her just the same way she always did and Tilly's funny feeling crept away. She was being silly. Of course her mum could see her. Imagine the trouble she'd have trying to buy shoes for an invisible Tilly!

'You're going to love it at school, Tilly,' said her mum, giving her a little hug.

'I know,' said Tilly. 'I just can't wait.'

Because once Tilly went to proper school like her brother and sisters everyone would just have to see how big she really was, wouldn't they?

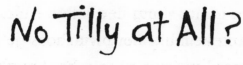

No Tilly at All?

Tilly's first morning at school got off to a wonderful start. They all went into the big hall and everyone sang a hymn called 'Morning Has Broken', which made her feel happily shivery inside.

A slanty bit of sunshine came in through the window while they were singing, making specks of dust dance like tiny angels. A bird flew past the window, its wings catching the light, and Tilly felt as if the whole world had been baked fresh overnight like a big new loaf of bread especially for her to bite into. Yum!

She gave a little skip as they followed Miss Hinchin back across the playground to the mobile classroom, admiring her own reflection in her shiny new shoes which still didn't quite feel like her own shoes yet.

I'm not little any more, she thought. I'm grown up now, and Tilly Beany gave a big sigh of happiness.

She patted her new shoe-bag as she went through the cloakroom, in case it was missing her. *Tilly Beany*, said the label on Tilly's peg in Miss Hinchin's big round teacher's writing, and there was the picture of the red umbrella.

'Summer suns are glowing,' Tilly hummed to herself, 'over land and sea.' That was the other song they had sung together in the big hall. She liked the idea of all those suns glowing away in the sky like rows of fiery marigolds.

After morning school was over she was going to Nathan's birthday party. It was going to be a lunch party instead of a tea party and all the children had to dress up as cowboys. What a day she was having!

'Now, I want each of you to paint a picture of yourselves,' Miss Hinchin said when they were back in the classroom. 'And I want you all to paint yourselves *exactly* the way you are.'

The children had to take it in turns to lie down while other children drew around them on big pieces of sugar paper, to get the size and shape right. Then they had to cut the body shapes out with little roundy-ended school scissors. That took quite a long time. Then everyone had to colour in his or her own picture.

Tilly couldn't wait for her turn. Steven and Natalie took ages to draw round her. They were slower than tortoises. For some reason Steven couldn't draw at all unless he stuck his tongue right out and breathed very hard. But Tilly was still the first to finish cutting out her shape. Her scissors danced round the edges of the paper like a pair of magic scissors. They didn't slip *once*. She couldn't wait to start painting. Every one of the colours had a different smell. The blue paint. The red. The yellow. Probably if you tasted them they had a different taste too.

'Summer suns are glowing,' Tilly hummed.

She didn't look round once to see what everyone else was doing, she was so excited that she could paint a picture of the real Tilly Beany at last! *Paint yourselves exactly the way you are*, Miss had said. Tilly had known school would be wonderful.

Miss Hinchin walked around the room smiling down at everyone's paintings. There was Emma in her dungarees and Pritesh in his new yellow jumper. Nathan was wearing his big birthday badge that said *I am Five*. Natalie had painted a red ribbon in her black curly hair instead of the real pink one because she didn't know how to make the colour pink yet, but Miss said that didn't matter at all.

Tilly smiled and smiled as Miss walked about the room. Her smile had just about reached her ears by the time Miss stopped beside her chair.

She was going to be amazed when she saw what Tilly had painted. But for some reason once she had looked at Tilly's painting Miss Hinchin wasn't smiling any more. She looked very surprised.

'Whatever have you done, Tilly?

Didn't you hear what I said?'

'Yes, Miss Hinchin,' said Tilly whose smile had somehow got stuck on to her face like a painted smile even though her smily feeling was fading very fast. 'You said to paint ourselves the way we really are. So I did,' she added.

'Stars?' said Miss Hinchin. 'Rainbows? Clouds with forked lightning coming out of them? Birds? Trees? Suns and moons and people dancing? Well, you have got a wonderful imagination, Tilly dear.'

Tilly's chin started to feel wobbly. Her eyes began to prickle. She had so loved those dancing people, all happily holding hands with each other.

Someone giggled. Soon most of the children were laughing. Nathan was laughing the loudest. Tilly crouched over her table so she didn't have to look at anybody. She wanted to put her fingers in her ears so she couldn't hear them either.

'It's who I really am,' she whispered to her painting. 'Inside.'

'I'll give you another piece of paper,' said Miss Hinchin kindly. 'Stop laughing, Nathan, that isn't very nice. Let's all help Tilly to do another picture so she can have one to put on the wall, the same as everyone else. Paint your lovely rosy cheeks, Tilly, and your beautiful shiny new shoes. That's what I wanted you to do. Perhaps you didn't understand, dear. Don't be upset. People often get themselves in a pickle when they're new. You'll soon get used to it.'

Tilly lay on the carpet as stiffly as a little stone girl, while Steven and Natalie slowly drew around her again. She could hear Steven breathing through his open mouth. It took about a hundred years. And when they finished, her scissors didn't dance around the edges of her paper this time. She cut slowly around the new empty Tilly shape. She couldn't really see it very well.

Her eyes felt too hot and prickly. She stuck
a brush in a pot of brown paint and painted
boring straight brown hair. She mixed up
some white and red paint and painted silly
rosy round cheeks. She stuck her brush in the
brown paint again to paint her new shoes.

And then she stopped. Dead.

If Miss Hinchin wasn't going to put
the real Tilly Beany on the wall, Miss
Hinchin wasn't going to have any Tilly
at all.

Tilly took hold of
the edges of her second
painting, tore it slowly right
across, twice, r-ip, r-ip, and

then she went to stand quietly by the door
to wait for her mum even though it was ten
minutes too early.

Miss Hinchin said she had never known
such a naughty new child.

Never.

And it was a very different Tilly waiting
silently by the classroom door when her
mum came to take her home at lunchtime.

'Hallo, Tilly, what did you do this
morning?' her mum asked her.

'Nothing,' said Tilly, staring at her new
shoes without seeing them, shutting her
mouth tight as tight. 'Nothing at all.'

'But Miss Hinchin is sticking up lots
of paintings on the wall,' said her mum,
puzzled. 'Everyone else has done lovely
big paintings of themselves. Didn't you do
one too?'

'Yes,' said Tilly fiercely, 'but mine was all
wrong. Don't talk about it.'

And she wouldn't say another word.

When they reached home she waited for her mum to unlock the front door then rushed straight upstairs where she shut herself in the bedroom she shared with her brother Tom. She banged the door so hard that little white flakes of plaster drifted down.

Tilly was never ever going to go to school again.

She could never tell anyone, not *anyone*, what had happened.

Tilly's face went red every time she thought about it. Every time she remembered how the other children had laughed, a spidery feeling crawled over her skin. How could she have made such a dreadful mistake?

Buffalo Stew

Sitting on her bed, waiting
miserably for it to be time for
Nathan's cowboy party, Tilly knew
that neither Kate nor Sophie, not
even her brother Tom, had ever been
so wicked on their first day at
school. And now she had to go to
the party and face all those children
who had laughed at her this
morning. But she wasn't going to let
them win. She was much, much too
big inside to do that. Tilly stared at
herself in the mirror on the little
white chest of drawers and her eyes
went very round and very green.

Later her mum called up the

18

stairs, 'Tilly! Time to get ready.'

When Tilly didn't answer, her mum thought she must have fallen asleep. Perhaps spending a whole morning at school had tired Tilly out after all.

'Time to get ready, Tilly,' she called again. There was still no reply. Tilly's mum came upstairs and knocked on the door.

'Tilly?'

Silence.

'Tilly!' Her mum twisted the doorknob and opened the door. 'What are you doing? I put your cowboy clothes on the –'

But there was no sign of Tilly anywhere.

Instead, gazing quietly out of the window was someone in bare feet wearing a fringed buckskin dress with a string of brightly coloured beads around her neck. There were glittery red and starry blue patterns painted on her face and her dark hair was tied round the forehead with a narrow strip of leather.

'I'm Windstar,' said the person calmly. 'And I'm a Native American princess. And I'm quite quite ready for the cowboy party, thank you.'

And the Native American princess smiled a calm princess's smile.

Tilly's mum didn't think it was wise for a Native American princess to turn up uninvited at a cowboy party, but she was in a big hurry to get the supermarket shopping done, so she didn't feel in the mood to argue. Besides, Windstar seemed so sure of herself.

And when Tilly's mum said, 'Don't you think it would be better if you wore the right clothes to the party?' Windstar only answered, 'But these *are* the right clothes for Native Americans,' and she said it so calmly and graciously that Tilly's mum felt rather silly. For some reason Windstar was much more polite than Tilly Beany. In fact, thought Tilly's mum, she was quite a restful change, though she worried that Windstar's feet would get cold on the way to the party. She needn't have bothered. Windstar found a large pair of moccasins at the last minute, right at the bottom of the old dressing-up box (underneath the furry bear suit Kate wore years ago, when she danced 'The Teddy Bears' Picnic' at Miss Violet Gladwell's ballet class).

'But I've got some much more *royal* ones at home,' Windstar said. 'With embroidery on. And beads.'

'Are you sure you really want to go to a cowboy party, Ti – Windstar?' asked Tilly's mum. 'Are you sure you won't feel just a bit nervous, being the only Native American with so many gun-toting cowboys around? Cowboys aren't usually very kind to your people, are they?'

Windstar thought about this seriously. 'Indians are very proud and they are very very brave,' she said at last. 'That's why

they *call* them "braves", you see,' she
added kindly.

'So you aren't worried,' said Tilly's mum.

'Not really,' said Windstar airily. 'Have
I got a birthday present to give Nathan?'

'Yes,' said Tilly's mum. 'I've wrapped it
up for you. I bought Nathan some Space
Lego.'

'It will have to do,' sighed Windstar.
'I would prefer to give him one of my wild
ponies but I don't expect Nathan would be
brave enough to ride bareback, and Native
American ponies can't stand to wear saddles
and bridles and all that stuff.'

As they opened the front door, Tilly's
mum did think Windstar looked the tiniest bit
pale under her red and blue glittery stars but
the Native American princess set off firmly
along the pavement, looking straight ahead
as if she didn't have a worry in the world.

It took longer than usual to get to
Nathan's house. The moccasins really were

very big and Windstar kept
walking out of them. But
by the time they reached
Nathan's front gate she
had found out
how to keep
them on by
squooshing her
bare toes down
hard inside the soft leather and
hanging on like a monkey, so she managed
to get all the way up the garden path
without them coming off once.

'Ti – Windstar,' said Tilly's mum as they
waited for Nathan's mum to open the door.
'Are you sure –?'

But the door flew open at that moment
and Nathan's mum stood smiling in the
doorway, wearing an enormous cowboy
hat and two pistols strapped on top of
her apron.

Something funny happened to her smile

when she caught sight of Windstar. She
looked quickly at Tilly's mum as if she
thought there might have been a mistake
but Tilly's mum said cheerfully, 'I'm afraid
Tilly couldn't come to Nathan's party, so
Windstar has come instead.'

'We meant to send smoke signals to let
you know,' said Windstar politely, 'but the
wood was damp.'

Just then Nathan came roaring up
waving a gun, screaming, 'Bang, zap,
kerpow,' then poked his head underneath his
mum's arm, trying to see what Tilly Beany
had brought him. Miles of torn-up birthday
paper trailed behind him. Windstar gripped
her parcel more tightly. Nathan was
wearing a black cowboy outfit that didn't
do up across his tummy. His face was very
red as if he had been running round
shouting, 'Kerpow, kerpow, bang, you're
dead!' at everyone for hours already.

Though she didn't know him yet, of

course, being a stranger from a foreign land, Windstar felt she might not like Nathan very much.

'Hey, this is a cowboy party,' Nathan said. 'Why are you dressed like that, silly Tilly? Si-lly Ti-lly got it wrong again!' he hooted.

'Oh, this isn't Tilly Beany, Nathan,' corrected his mum. 'Tilly couldn't come. This little girl is Windstar, the Native American princess.'

Nathan's smile faded. He looked puzzled.

Windstar handed over her parcel. 'Sorry I couldn't bring you the wild pony,' she said with a very small smile. 'I was afraid you wouldn't be strong and fierce enough to ride it.'

Nathan's mum managed to say, 'Well, please come in – Wind – sorry, I didn't quite catch your name?'

'Windstar,' said the princess firmly.

'Please come in, Windstar. I hope you won't find it uncomfortable to be surrounded by so many cowboys, but we weren't actually expecting any – any of your people. We'll do our best to make you feel at home.'

'Don't worry about me,' said Windstar. 'I am very brave.'

By this time there was a crowd of cowboys and cowgirls, some clutching pistols and lassoes, gathering round Nathan's mum, staring in astonishment at the mysterious new visitor.

'May I leave my moccasins by the door, please?' asked Windstar. She had walked out of them again. Holding them on with monkey toes was getting tiring.

'Of course,' said Nathan's mum. 'Then perhaps you'd like to come and share Nathan's birthday lunch with us.'

'Thank you,' said Windstar. 'I will *try* some to be polite. But I'm not sure cowboy

food would be suitable for my insides. What do cowboys eat?'

'Well, *these* cowboys are eating burgers, bangers and beans,' said Nathan's mum. 'Apart from the vegetarian ones,' she added with a sigh. 'What do the people of your tribe eat, mainly?'

Windstar thought hard, her forehead crinkling. 'You mean apart from roots, berries, wild honey and things like that?'

'Apart from things like that,' agreed Nathan's mum. She was having trouble with her cowboy hat. It was too big. Suddenly she took it off and dumped it on the hall table.

'Buffalo stew,' announced Windstar. 'On special occasions we eat buffalo stew. Around the fire.'

Nathan giggled but Windstar gave him a cool proud look and he stopped at once, the way he never would have done for Tilly.

'Then of course I'll try to find you

some,' said Nathan's mum, kindly. 'But it might take a little time to prepare.'

'Oh, it does,' agreed Windstar. 'Days and days. Where is the party, please?'

'It's in here,' said Nathan rushing ahead to show the way. 'Mum and Dad have done it all up. It's great.'

Windstar stalked through a pair of folding doors into the dining room which now looked like a saloon bar out of a TV western. Everyone trailed after her. Some of the children who had been clutching pistols let them slip out of their hands, as if they couldn't quite remember why they'd been holding them.

There was a big sign over the dining table. Windstar peered at it.

'That says "Dodge City Diner",' explained Nathan. Nathan's mum had filled the enormous saucepan she usually used for making jam with baked beans and tiny sausages and Nathan's big sister Becky was dishing up platefuls of cowboy food for everyone.

Another sister with bright pink ostrich feathers in her hair, wearing a tight, shiny, blue dress that showed a lot of her front, was banging out a honky-tonk tune on the piano. The piano had a handwritten sign on it too.

'That one says "Miss Amy's Saloon". Amy's the saloon bar lady,' said Nathan. 'And we're going to play "Pin the Badge on the Sheriff", and after dinner we're

DODGE CITY
DINER

having a treasure hunt but it's called a "Gold Rush" and if you find any gold you can take it home. It's only chocolate money really,' he added nervously. 'Mum hid it. I wasn't allowed to watch.'

Windstar stood silently staring around her, unsmiling. It was impossible to tell what she was thinking because Native American princesses always keep their faces so blank, but she didn't look terribly impressed. The children felt uncomfortable. Suddenly it didn't seem so much fun to dash around *powing* each other.

'I think I'll just sit here and watch you all,' Windstar said at last. 'And wait for my buffalo stew to be ready.'

She seated herself on the ground, cross-legged, and stared straight ahead of her.

'I'll wait with you, Windstar,' said Stephanie. 'I don't want to be a cowboy any more. I think it's silly. I'd much rather be a Native American like you.'

30

And Stephanie took her cowboy hat off and sat down beside Windstar and crossed *her* legs, and stared straight ahead too.

'Isn't *anybody* going to come and eat their dinner?' called Nathan's sister Becky rather desperately. 'If you don't eat your dinner, you can't have the birthday cake.'

Several children dashed away, then turned around at the last minute and drifted back to hang around Windstar again.

'Native Americans are very, very wise, aren't they, Windstar?' said Stephanie softly, as if they were all by themselves and not surrounded by cowboys.

'Very wise,' agreed Windstar. 'I've got some face paints in my pocket. Would you like me to paint your face like mine, Stephanie, and give you your Native American name, then you can be one too?'

'Oh, yes,' said Stephanie.

'There aren't many Native Americans left alive in our time,' said Windstar in a louder voice, 'because the cowboys killed them and took their land away. But people can change back *into* Native Americans if they really want to. I'm going to paint two little flowers on you and then your Native American name can be Two Flowers.'

By the time Nathan's mum came in with the buffalo stew, Windstar and Two Flowers were busily painting the faces of two other children and there was a small queue waiting to be made into Native American too. At the other end of the room Nathan and the rest of his friends stood scowling in their cowboy clothes.

'It's fun being a Native American, Nathan,' said Stephanie sunnily. 'Do you want to try next? I'll paint you if you like.'

But Nathan only backed further away, his arms folded across his chest, muttering to himself.

No one was eating the cowboy food. Becky had given up trying to make them

Tilly Beany.

'Well, sometimes,' she said slowly, 'sometimes we have a tug of war.'

'*That's* a good idea, Nathan, isn't it?' said Nathan's mum brightly. She was looking rather tired. 'I'm sure Daddy's got a strong piece of rope in the garage. The cowboys and Native Americans can have a tug of war. *That* would be exciting.'

'Can I stop playing the piano now?' asked Miss Amy, hobbling over in her shiny dress. 'My fingers are killing me and I'm starving. That face paint looks fun. Will you paint me, Stephanie, when you've finished with Ben?'

'Goodness,' said Tilly's mum when she came to collect Windstar from the party. 'Where did you get all those gold coins?'

Windstar trudged and squooshed along happily in her big moccasins. A falling leaf came whirling down through the air.

Windstar caught it as it spun past and it was golden too.

'I won them,' she said. 'We had a tug of war between the cowboys and the Native Americans, and the Native Americans won, of course.'

Tilly's mum was puzzled. 'But I thought you were the only Native American at Nathan's party,' she said.

'Not in the end I wasn't,' said Windstar mysteriously. 'Not in the *end*.'

Oats and Beans and Barley Grow

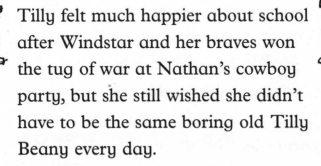

Tilly felt much happier about school after Windstar and her braves won the tug of war at Nathan's cowboy party, but she still wished she didn't have to be the same boring old Tilly Beany every day.

'Boring!' said her dad, at breakfast. 'You must be *joking*. I haven't had a dull moment since you were born, Jellybean. I haven't had nearly enough boring moments if you really want to know. I never know what you're going to do next.'

'Don't you?' said Tilly, surprised. 'Well, I'm going to school, actually, Daddy. I thought you'd know that. I've been going every day for *ages*.'

'Ah yes, but which Tilly is going to school,' he teased. 'That's what I never know.'

'Just the usual one,' she said sadly. 'Miss Hinchin said it was much too cold for Windstar to come.'

'Poor Windstar,' said Tilly's dad. 'And she was such a nice polite girl. I did like her.'

That week Tilly's school were having their Harvest Festival. Tilly took a big tin of spaghetti hoops, a huge marrow from her dad's allotment and a jar of her mum's home-made blackberry jelly. Tilly felt rather worried about taking the jelly. Home-made blackberry jelly was her favourite food in the world, especially with peanut butter. She didn't want the Beanys to run out. But she counted the jars left behind in the larder and it seemed quite a lot.

On the day the mums and dads were

invited to come in to the school Tilly's mum was too busy, so Tilly's dad had the morning off work especially to see Tilly do her Wheat Dance. She'd been practising it for *weeks*.

First Steven was the farmer planting the seeds while everyone sang 'Oats and Beans and Barley Grow', then while Miss Hinchin played a dreamy piece of music called 'Morning' on the tape recorder, Tilly, Alice and Shazna had to be the corn growing slowly up and up in their rustling golden headdresses, stretching out their ripening stalks to the sun and the rain, swaying and bowing.

Then Nathan, Darren and Pritesh came along in a pretend combine harvester to cut the corn. Tilly thought Nathan enjoyed the cutting down part much too much. She could hear him muttering, 'Whack, whack, whack,' as he stomped along the rows in his baggy farmer's dungarees and big black

wellington boots. He cut
it much too fast, too.

Tilly liked being the
waving corn swaying
gracefully in the sun.
She never wanted that
part to end. She felt
like a real ballet
dancer. The music
was so beautiful that
she almost felt
beautiful herself
while she was
dancing to it. Tilly
badly wanted her

dad to see how beautiful and dancery she
was. So this morning Tilly waited until
Nathan was standing right in front of her,
still hissing, 'Whack, whack,' through his
teeth, but instead of falling to the ground
the way she was supposed to, she whispered,
'Buffalo stew.'

Nathan went bright red and stomped right past her, completely forgetting to cut down Tilly's corn.

Alice and Shazna were lying on the carpet with their eyes closed by this time so Tilly swayed around beautifully all by herself, just the way she'd always wanted to, humming along with the music.

Miss Hinchin was waving anxiously at her from behind the piano to make her lie down like the other girls, but Tilly wasn't in a hurry. She could see her daddy in the second row, all squashed on to a tiny school chair, next to Shazna's mum and dad, and he was smiling.

At last, but only when she felt perfectly ready, Tilly sank to the floor with her hand on her heart, looking terribly sad. Tilly was sure corn didn't enjoy being cut down one bit. She thought it was silly of Alice to grin the whole time she was dancing. Alice actually *waved* at her mum!

'Did you see me?' Tilly asked as soon as she met her daddy at the door. 'Was I good?'

'You were wonderful,' said Tilly's dad. 'The most beautiful corn I've ever seen in my life. But before we go home for lunch, Jellybean, I've just got to pop into the office for a minute.'

Witchworks

'Hurray!' said Tilly. Tilly liked it when her daddy called her Jellybean and she liked going to work with her dad. She liked the way Greta's hoop earrings and golden bracelets jangled when she was typing and the way she said, 'Hallo, who's calling? Hold the line *one* moment, please,' in a special soft secretary's voice when she answered the phone.

Today, before Tilly went home, Greta let her sit in her swivelly secretary's chair, and gave her a little pad of notepaper, some paper clips and some sticky labels to take home with her.

'You'll be able to set up your

43

own office now, Tilly,' laughed Greta.

'What's your office *for*, Daddy?' Tilly asked as they drove home.

'We're an agency. We put people in touch with other people,' said her dad. 'That's the simplest way of describing it. If people want a salesman we find them a salesman. But we don't just have salesmen on our books. And if what they really want –'

Tilly sat hugging her knees, enjoying listening to her daddy's voice telling her grown-up things. She never understood any of it when he explained but it didn't matter. It sounded very busy and important and she liked that. She wished she was grown-up and could rush around saying, 'Not now, I'm too busy.' Or, 'Who's calling? Hold the line please.'

Children could never say *they* were busy. Even if they were right in the middle of something grown-ups could always interrupt them, just because it was bedtime or dinner or time to go out to the shops. As if nothing children did was ever the least bit important.

For some reason Tilly didn't understand, only grown-ups and big children with homework were allowed to say they were busy.

'Not now, Tilly,' Kate and Sophie would say. 'I'm too busy. I've got *loads* of homework. Go and ask Tom.'

Tom wasn't old enough to be busy either. But he would be soon and that would leave Tilly all by herself again.

Tilly sighed. Her dad was still explaining about his office. He liked talking about work. She decided she'd heard enough now and after a while she interrupted.

'Daddy, what else is there, after Harvest Festival and before Christmas?'

'What else? Oh, lots of things,' said her dad. 'There's Halloween with all the witches and pumpkins. Then there's November and fireworks.'

'Oh yes! Witches and fireworks. Witches and fireworks,' Tilly chanted. She chanted the words to herself over and over until she got in a muddle and started saying, 'Fires and witchworks.'

'Witchworks,' said her dad, laughing. 'That's a good word. It sounds like a very magic kind of office – even more magic than mine, Tilly!'

'It is,' said Tilly at once. 'That's *exactly* what it is. We put people in touch with whatever is the right kind of magic for them. We don't just have witches on our books, actually. If people want a witch, we find them a witch. But if they feel worried by the idea of witches or they think flying carpets are a bit too *sudden*, we just give them the phone number of a really reliable genie.'

'Wonderful,' said Tilly's dad, parking the car. 'Could you rustle up a genie to make us some scrambled eggs for lunch, Jellybean, do you think?'

Tilly shook her head, laughing. 'Genies just like to move castles about and that sort of thing.'

But Tilly Beany looked very thoughtful while she was eating her eggs and her eyes went very round and very green indeed, and after lunch she disappeared for a long, long time.

'Where's Tilly?' asked Tilly's mum when she came home.

'Don't know,' said Sophie crossly. She was practising her clarinet and that always made her cross.

'In the garage, I think,' yawned Kate who was watching *Blue Peter* and doing her maths homework at the same time.

'In the dark?' said Tilly's mum. 'She'll freeze to death. Whatever is she doing down there?'

But when Tilly's mum reached the

bottom of the garden she could see right away that the Beany's garage was not a garage any more.

Someone had cleared a big space and swept it carefully clean. In the middle of this space there was a little light glimmering and behind a table someone was talking in a specially soft voice into a telephone, while she sorted busily through a little pile of papers with her other hand.

'Witchworks,' said the someone. 'Can I help you? Who's calling? What service do you require? Fortune telling? Oh, you've already seen our fortune teller. And you didn't *like* the fortune. Oh dear, I am sorry. *Seven* children. All with measles at the same time. That's terrible. Well, of course you could have your money back or maybe we could find you a fortune teller you'd like better. Would you rather try our wizard instead? He is supposed to be *very* good.'

The person behind the desk put down the phone and sighed as if she was having a difficult day. Then she saw Tilly's mum and smiled a very charming smile.

'Good afternoon,' she said politely. 'Can I help you?' The lady was wearing a pair of extremely high-heeled shoes, and perched on the end of her nose was a pair of round gold glasses that didn't seem to have any glass in them. When the lady moved, the bracelets on her arms jangled like soft music. The lady seemed to enjoy jangling them.

'I don't know,' said Tilly's mum. 'Actually I was rather surprised to find this office in our – down here.

Is this a new business?'

'Yes, rather new. We specially wanted to be open in time for Halloween. Is there anything I can do for you? Tom hasn't –' The lady looked cross for a moment and then corrected herself, '*We* haven't had time to put up the proper sign yet, but when it's ready it will say WITCHWORKS – MAGIC AT YOUR SERVICE. We do spells, charms, anything that's a bit magic.'

'How wonderful!' said Tilly's mum. 'But at the moment I'm looking for my little girl, Tilly. It's almost her teatime.'

'Sorry,' said the lady, scribbling busily on a pad. 'We don't look for lost children. You can hire a flying carpet and look for her yourself, if you like.'

She pointed to a little roll of carpet at her side. It was pink and flowery and tied up with string and Tilly's mum remembered seeing something surprisingly like it in her own boxroom a few days ago, next to the dressing-up box.

'I don't think so,' said Tilly's mum. 'It looks rather small. I don't think there would be enough room on it for me to bring Tilly back when I find her.'

'You could hire two,' the lady pointed out.

'Have you got two?' said Tilly's mum, looking around.

'Not yet,' admitted the lady. 'But we might have by tomorrow.'

'I think I'd like my Tilly back a little bit sooner than tomorrow,' said Tilly's mum firmly.

The lady frowned to herself as if she was thinking hard and pushed her glasses back on her nose. 'Maybe we could help you just this once,' she said. 'If you really are very very worried.'

Then she made a soft ringing sound to herself, 'Drring, drring,' and picked up the telephone. 'Hallo? Is that Titch the witch? You finished all the spells early today?

51

Well, I might have another job for you.
There's a lady here who's looking for a
little girl. I told her we don't usually – All
right. You'll do it? I'll tell her you're
coming. Bye.'

The lady put the phone down and
smiled charmingly at Tilly's mum again.
'Titch the witch will come to your house
quite soon and see if she can help you find
your little girl.'

'Thank you,' said Tilly's mum
gratefully. 'Would she like some tea when
she arrives, do you know?'

'Oh, I expect she'd like a little snack,'
said the lady. 'But I'd better warn you she
does prefer everything quite green.'

Tilly's mum went back up the garden
smiling to herself.

Just then Tom came out of the house
carrying a large piece of cardboard with
some big black writing on it.

'Where's Tilly?' he said. 'She asked me

to write a sign for her office.'

'I don't quite know where *Tilly* is at the moment,' said Mum. 'But I do want you all to keep extremely calm. A witch is coming for tea tonight.'

By six o'clock the table was laid and the mashed potatoes were ready but still the witch had not appeared. Everyone wondered *how* she would arrive. Sophie giggled that she would probably fly down the chimney on her broomstick. Kate thought she'd burst in through the French windows jabbering spells.

'Perhaps she'll appear in the middle of the room in a puff of green smoke,' joked Tom.

But as the time ticked past and the potatoes grew colder, the family became rather nervous.

Suddenly there was a ring at the doorbell and everyone jumped.

'I'll get it,' said Sophie, giggling again.

But when she opened the door she stopped giggling straight away. In fact she gasped with surprise.

Titch the witch was worth waiting for. She was witchy all right. She was splendidly witchy all over. Her hat, her dress, her swirly cloak were as black as midnight. Her face and her hands were as green as pondweed. Even some of the straggly hair that peeped out from underneath her hat was green.

'Please come in,' said Sophie, backing away, hoping none of the green would come off on *her*.

'Your mother is expecting me,' said the witch, staring past Sophie in an unfriendly way.

Titch the witch had a witchy voice too.
Cross and crabby.

'We all are,' said Sophie. 'We've never had a witch for tea before.'

'I haven't come for tea,' said the witch sternly. 'I've come for business and I'm having an extremely busy day so I can't waste time talking to *you*, Sophie.'

'Sorry,' said Sophie in a small voice.

The witch sat herself right down in Tilly's chair without being invited.

'What's your problem?' she said in a cross, sandpapery voice.

'We need to find Tilly,' said Tilly's mum. 'The lady at Witchworks said you might help us.'

'Of course I can,' said the witch. 'I know where she is right now this minute.'

'Well, do you think you could tell us, please?' asked Tilly's dad. 'She'll be very cold and hungry, and she ought to be home for her tea by now.'

'Tilly's busy,' said the witch. 'Very, very busy and can't be disturbed.' The witch was looking at the bowl of mashed potatoes. 'Haven't you got anything green to eat?' she grumbled. 'Green food helps me think.'

'Well, some of it's *quite* green,' said Mum. 'The peas are very green and there is a green jelly for pudding.'

'That will do,' said the witch rudely. 'I'll have peas and jelly.'

Sophie giggled again but Tilly's big sister Kate had noticed how tired the witch was looking, now she was sitting down in the warm cosy room. In fact, from the strange faces the witch had started to pull, Kate thought she might be trying hard not to yawn.

'There's parsley on the potatoes,' said Dad. 'That's green.'

'I'll have some of them too,' said the witch.

'And if you put a little mint sauce on the lamb,' said Kate kindly, 'that would be green too, wouldn't it?'

'All right,' said the witch. She held out her plate but before she could start to eat she yawned after all, a very big, very loud yawn. She clapped her hand fiercely over her mouth before another yawn could sneak out.

'Have you been busy making spells all day, poor thing?' said Kate sympathetically.

'Yes,' snapped the witch glaring at her. 'I am a very busy person.'

'What kind of spells were they?'

'Secret spells,' said the witch cunningly. 'People have to pay me for my spells. I don't give them away for nothing.'

'Have you got a homework spell?' Kate asked. 'I'd love a spell that could do my maths homework for me.'

'I expect a really reliable genie could do it for you,' said the witch, yawning again. 'You should ask the lady at Witchworks.'

'I will,' promised Kate. 'Thank you.'

A few minutes later, Titch the witch fell

asleep right in the middle of her green jelly. All at once her head fell forward and she started to snore. She had only eaten one tiny spoonful.

'She really is an awfully small witch,' said Tilly's mum. 'I think she's stayed out way past her bedtime.'

'Perhaps if we put her to sleep in Tilly's bed,' said Dad, lifting the witch up in his arms so that her hat fell off, carrying her gently towards the stairs, 'we'll find Tilly there in the morning.'

'Ah well,' said Tilly's mum, picking up the tall witchy hat with the green spiky hair still glued to it, 'who knows *who* we'll find in Tilly's bed in the morning!'

Matilda Seaflower

It was half-term and the Beany family were going to stay with Great Aunt Rose, who lived by the sea. Tilly was bursting with excitement. This was the first interesting thing to happen to the Beany family since Titch the witch came to tea.

'It's not the most sensible time of year to visit the seaside,' said Tilly's dad as they drove down. 'But it will make a nice change. And it's a beautiful day.'

Tilly didn't remember the seaside. The last time the Beanys made the trip she was too tiny to notice anything. But this time, from

60

the moment Tilly's mum wound down the window and said, 'Oh, Tilly, smell the sea,' Tilly was perched on the very edge of her seat, gazing and gazing, determined to notice *everything*.

There were strange silky yellow flowers by the side of the road. Her mum said they were sea poppies. Tilly had always thought all poppies were red, the way they were at home.

So there were sea flowers as well as land flowers. Tilly remembered that there were sea people, too, called mermaids. They didn't have legs like land people. They had tails like fishes and sang out on the rocks when it was wild and stormy. She wished she could see one, just one mermaid, before she went home again.

Even the grass was different here. Rough and wiry-looking. There was a thin white cottage like a pointy finger sticking out of the water meadows by itself. As they drove past Tilly saw that its walls were decorated with shells and pebbles just as if the mermaids had swum up the river in the night and put them there for fun. It looked so special and magic, Tilly hoped this might be Aunt Rose's house, but her mum said it wasn't. And soon there were more houses and all painted such dazzling colours it hurt Tilly's eyes to look at them in the bright sunlight.

Then all at once they saw the sea and it was better than Tilly had ever dreamed; moving and changing the whole time, sometimes blue, sometimes grey and silver, but always much too bright to look at for long and far too big to take in all at once. And every inch of it was alive and busy with tiny white waves.

There was even a bright, white ship too, sailing into the distance. Tilly thought she would burst with happiness.

They were early so Tilly's dad said they

would park the car and walk down to the
sea, just to say hallo. As they got out of the
car a seagull gave its loud shrill call as it
went sailing above their heads. Tilly almost
jumped out of her skin. Sea birds seemed
fiercer than land birds.

'That bird's
beak is too big,'
she said. 'I hope it
won't try to bite me.'

But secretly she
liked the lonely sound
it made. It belonged
with the dazzling
houses, the yellow
poppies, and the
salty whipping
wind. Tilly's
mum made
Tilly fasten
her anorak right
up to the chin.

To reach the sea they had to walk past a row of small shops. Even the shops had different things in the windows. Tiny sailing boats. Boxes decorated with shells. Funny hats with messages written on them. Kate and Sophie giggled over the hats but Tilly couldn't read what they said. There were sweets like walking sticks, and sweets like enormous babies' dummies made of bright red sugar. Tilly thought it would be nice to have one to suck but people might think she was still a baby if she asked for one.

Kate and Sophie didn't want to walk down to the sea. They said it was so cold they'd get earache and anyway they were wearing the wrong sort of shoes. They wanted to go in all the shops instead.

Tilly's mum said they could have a quick look in *one* of the shops, then they would all go down to the sea together because it was a family holiday and that was that.

Kate and Sophie dived straight into the shop with the loudest music coming out of it and everyone else followed them inside rather gloomily. They had to stay in there for ages. Tilly thought she'd die. Even through the noise of the pop song, Tilly could hear the waves swooshing and swishing. The sea was calling her name. *'Tillee – ssh – Tillee – ssh . . .'*

And then she saw the mermaid's mirror.

Tilly knew what it was at once. It had that silvery-green shimmer only a truly magic thing could have and it looked so exactly like the mirrors mermaids have in books. It had a long handle, like the stalk of a flower, and a round glass part for the mermaid to look in and comb her hair, and it was decorated all over with the tiniest pearliest shells Tilly had ever seen in her life. She began to tug at once at her mum's sleeve. 'Mum . . .'

'Just a minute, Tilly, and I promise we'll go down to the sea.'

'No, *look*, Mum. It's a mermaid's mirror. She must have lost it in a storm. Look.'

'So it is, Tilly,' said her mum, still not looking properly.

'Can I have it? Please?'

'Tilly, what would you do with a mirror? It would be broken after five minutes. We'll buy some sweets for everyone to share, then you can collect some lovely shells for nothing down on the beach.'

Her mum didn't understand, Tilly thought. She had to have that mirror. It was a mermaid's mirror and she couldn't leave it in this loud dark shop with all the silly summer seaside things. The mermaid would be looking everywhere for it.

She tried her dad.

'Dad – I've found a real mermaid's mirror!'

'That's lovely, Tilly. Is everybody ready?

What about some humbugs to warm us up on the beach?'

Kate and Sophie were buying tons of things with their own money. It wasn't fair. Tilly only had thirty pence a week. She would have to save up for her whole life if she wanted to buy the mirror and someone else would have bought it by then. Her eyes filled with tears.

'What's wrong, Jellybean?' Tom came up beside her and, surprisingly, squeezed her hand. 'Cheer up, Till, we're going down to the sea now and we can go on the beach every day until we go home. I don't care how cold it is, do you? Aunt Rose's house is only a few yards away. Hey, we'll be able to hear it at night. I love that sound.'

Tilly was afraid to speak in case she burst out howling like a baby, so she just pointed to the mirror and a big tear crawled down her nose.

'What's the matter, Tilly?'

'It's a mermaid's,' she whispered. 'A mermaid's mirror. It doesn't want to stay in this shop and be bought by someone horrible.'

Tom understood. That was the thing about Tom. Mostly he was too awful for words. But sometimes, just sometimes, he understood things absolutely no one else did.

'Mum, Dad,' he shouted. 'Tilly's found a mermaid's mirror. If she doesn't ask for anything else all the holiday, couldn't she have it? I'll give some of my pocket money towards it.'

That was the other thing about Tom. He didn't talk much. So when he spoke people took him seriously. But Tilly chattered away all the time so no one listened to her at all!

As she watched the lady carefully wrap the mermaid's mirror in some not very nice green paper, Tilly swore that from now on she was going to be just like Tom and only talk when she absolutely had to, then everyone would listen to *her*.

Sophie was sulking loudly. 'It's not fair. Tilly always gets her own way, just because she's the littlest. She's spoilt!'

Tilly was furious. She opened her mouth to yell back that if Sophie thought it was so brilliant being little she could swap with her right now. And anyway, she was going to shout, it was a mirror, a real magic mirror. There mightn't ever be another chance . . . And then she remembered just in time that from now on she was going to be quiet, just like Tom, and she snapped her mouth tight shut again.

'Happy now, Jellybean?' asked her dad, holding out the bag of humbugs.

She nodded, took the sweet and popped

it in her mouth. It was easy to practise not talking when you were sucking a humbug. She clutched her parcel tightly. Even through the shiny green paper she could feel how magic it was. A magic mirror and Tilly was holding it in her very own hands.

'Oh,' said Kate excitedly. 'The tide's out! Look at the rocks. I love rock pools. Bet I find a crab.'

And just as if they had never said the beach was cold and boring, Tilly's big sisters went racing off down the sand, shrieking with laughter, the wind whipping their long dark hair.

Tilly badly wanted long hair. Her mum said she could grow hers when she was old enough to wash it all by herself. She pulled the ends hard. It wasn't *that* short. But it was rather brown. She seemed to remember that mermaids had fair hair. Maybe not *all* of them.

Suddenly, Tom grabbed her hand and

began tugging her really fast over the wet
sand towards the sea, so that she shrieked
at the top of her voice, just like Sophie and
Kate, and spat her humbug out by mistake.

But she didn't mind. It was too hot and
bulgy to fit in her mouth unless she
concentrated hard and she wanted every bit
of her attention for the sea. While the others
clambered about on the slippery rocks,
chasing each other with dripping black
seaweed and putting handfuls of shells in
their pockets, Tilly just stood and stared and
stared at the sea. It was the most amazing

thing she had ever seen in her life! Yet she felt as if she already knew it very well. And the sea knew her too and whispered its secrets to her.

'*Tillee – ssh – Tillee – ssh . . .*' it sang as it danced up to her feet and went dancing back, sucking the tiny stones with it, '*. . . sssh . . . Tillee . . .*'

'Tell her,' Tilly whispered back into the wind. 'Tell her I've got her mirror and I'll keep it very, very safe.'

The sea would tell the mermaid about Tilly and Tilly would give the mirror back. She didn't mind at all. If she could only once see a real live mermaid swim up out of the sea and comb her long hair and sing her sad song beside the rock pool, she would never mind about anything ever again.

She was so thoughtful while her dad was driving them to Aunt Rose's house that her mum said, 'We really must come to the seaside more often. I've never known Tilly so mousy quiet. It must be the sea air.'

Tilly liked Aunt Rose. She had a crinkly smile that made Tilly beam right back. She liked Aunt Rose's house, too, even if it wasn't as magic as the lonely cottage with the shell-patterned walls. She liked the bedroom she had to share with Tom and her sisters, because she could see the sea out of the window, and she liked the lovely shepherd's pie Aunt Rose gave them for supper, but she didn't really notice much else. All the rest of the day Tilly was puzzling about how she could manage to meet the mermaid. Mermaids were very shy, she knew, and probably they were terribly upset about the cruel things people did to seals and whales. That's why people hardly ever saw mermaids any more. Like fairies. However could Tilly get a frightened little mermaid to trust her?

'I seem to remember that when Tilly was a baby she bellowed at the top of her voice the whole time,' said Great Aunt Rose. 'But we've hardly heard a squeak from her all evening. Isn't it amazing how children change!'

'Amazing,' agreed Tilly's dad.

'Can I play in the garden, Aunt Rose,' asked Tom. 'Before we go to bed?'

Tilly followed him outside.

'Hey, Tilly,' Tom said. 'Want a ride in Aunt Rose's wheelbarrow?'

'If you promise not to tip me out,' said Tilly.

She noticed something. 'What's that green stuff?'

'The netting? Aunt Rose uses it for her sweet peas to climb up.'

'Do you think she needs it any more?' asked Tilly thoughtfully and her eyes went very round and very green.

'Tilly,' said Tom. 'What are you planning?'

'Tom,' said Tilly in her softest, nicest voice. 'Do you think you could help me?

You'd have to get up
very early, before anyone
else is awake . . .'

But old ladies wake
early too and when Aunt
Rose looked out of her
window next morning
she was surprised to see Tom trundling her
wheelbarrow over the beach towards the
sea. And for a moment she *thought* she saw
the strangest little figure perched inside it.

Almost like – but it
couldn't be!

'Good heavens,'
she murmured,
rubbing her
spectacles on a little cloth to clean them. 'I
must be imagining things,' she said aloud.

'Where's Tilly?' asked Tilly's dad at
breakfast. 'Is she still asleep?'

'N – o,' said Tom. 'I don't think so.'

'Is she in the garden?' asked Tilly's mum.

'N – o,' said Tom, 'not really.'

'Tom,' said Sophie. 'You can't fool us. You're up to something fishy.'

Tom started to laugh. 'I'm not,' he said. 'But someone else is. *Very* fishy indeed.'

'I bet I know who,' said Kate and she stood up with a big sigh. 'Mum,' she said. 'What do you think mermaids eat for breakfast?'

'Oh, no,' groaned her dad. 'Don't tell me.'

'Tilly,' called Kate as she went running across the sand with Aunt Rose's shopping bag in her arms. 'Tilly Beany!'

But as she got closer, she saw that the strange little person sitting dreamily all by herself beside a rock pool, combing her hair and gazing into a beautiful mirror, was not Tilly Beany at all.

'Ssh,' hissed the person very crossly. 'She'll never come out of the sea and sing to

me if you shout. And I'm not Tilly Beany
anyway. I'm Matilda Seaflower and I'm
a mermaid too. Go away, Kate. You'll spoil
everything.'

'So what's this?' asked Kate, prodding
the mermaid's lower half.

'My tail, silly,' said Matilda Seaflower.
'Careful or you'll unwind it. I've got to be
a mermaid or she'll be much too scared to
come out of the sea to get her mirror back.

Mermaids are frightened of land people. Don't you know anything?'

'Your hair's a bit short,' said Kate. 'For a mermaid.'

'It isn't,' the mermaid snapped. 'It's growing extremely fast, actually. This is a magic mirror and the comb's magic too, anyway, and by night-time my hair will be all the way down to here, so there.' She pointed to her waist. 'Look, it's longer already.'

'You're right,' said Kate, kindly. 'Sorry. I like the yellow flower in it though. But it's falling out a tiny bit. Let me fix it for you. Aren't you a little bit cold, Matilda? Wouldn't you like to put this nice cosy jumper on?'

'Mermaids don't get cold.'

Kate thought the little mermaid's face looked a bit blue but perhaps that was normal for mermaids.

'What about hungry?' asked Kate

cunningly. 'Don't mermaids eat breakfast either?'

There was a little pause, then Matilda said cautiously, 'Sometimes.'

'I made a special sandwich, you see, just in case I met a hungry mermaid when I came out this morning,' Kate went on. 'A special sandwich with the kind of things in it mermaids like best. Delicious things. It smells lovely. The cat went absolutely wild while I was making it. But I disguised it to look like a blackberry jelly and peanut butter sandwich, so no one would guess where I was going.'

'I'm not coming indoors, Kate,' said the little mermaid in Tilly's voice, gobbling down the sandwich very fast. 'I'm not coming inside that house ever again until I've given this mirror back to the poor little mermaid.'

'Oh,' said Kate. She could see that this might take a very long time indeed. And

Matilda had turned *very* blue. Even for a mermaid.

'Suppose,' she said, 'suppose I told you a magic way to ask the other mermaid if she really wants her mirror back.'

'Of course she does. It's so beautiful. She must be so upset,' said Matilda, looking rather unhappy herself.

'A very magic way,' repeated Kate. 'Don't you even want to try it?'

Matilda frowned. 'I don't know.'

Her teeth were chattering so hard now that if Matilda hadn't been a mermaid Kate might have thought she was *freezing*.

Kate was hunting around in the sand.

'Got it!' she said. She dug up a big wet cockleshell with her fingers and carefully shook the sand out of it.

'Put this to your ear, Matilda,' she said. 'And listen very hard.'

'What to?'

'Just listen. It's a sea telephone.

Mermaids use them all the time.'

The little mermaid stuck the big shell close to her ear. 'I can't understand what they're saying,' she said, looking so upset Kate was afraid she might burst out crying. 'They're whispering too softly to me.'

'Maybe you've got a wrong number,' said Kate. 'Let's see if I can do it.' She took the shell and held it to her ear. She smiled suddenly. 'Hallo,' she said. 'I was afraid you were out. It's nice to talk to you. This is Kate Beany, Tilly's sister. Yes, she's found your mirror. Isn't it wonderful! I thought you'd be pleased. She wants to know what to do with it.'

Matilda's eyes had grown enormous.

Kate was still listening. 'Can you speak up?' she said. 'This line isn't very good. Some extra large whales must have got in the way. Oh, okay. Fine. That's lovely. That's what we'll do then. Bye.'

She replaced the shell telephone in the

sand and carefully placed some tiny pink shells beside it. 'Mermaids use these for money,' she explained.

'What did she say?'

'She wants you to ask the sea to deliver the mirror to her house in the Underwater City. She says she's sorry but she's much too shy to come out of the water to meet you, even though you are another mermaid. But she says thank you very much for looking after it for her.'

'Oh dear,' said the little mermaid, shivering. 'How will I get down to the waves? I'll have to wriggle ever so far on my tummy.'

The tide was out a very long way.

'I'll carry you,' said Kate. 'Don't worry. Goodness, your tail's prickly, Matilda.'

'I know,' said the little mermaid. 'Sorry. That's just how it grew.'

Matilda Seaflower let Kate carry her all the way down to the sea's edge. Only a little

bit of tail got left behind. Kate was very
careful with it.

'Can the mermaid see me really?'
Matilda asked. 'Are you sure, Kate?'

'Yes,' said Kate, carefully watching the
waves as they came dancing in. 'I know she
can. She's got a special magic window and
when she looks
through it
she can see
everything that
happens on the
seashore. There's
a big wave
coming – *Now*,
Matilda!'

As the giant
wave rushed in, Matilda Seaflower bravely
tossed the mermaid's mirror into the green
swirling water.

'Please, sea, take the mirror to the
Underwater City,' she called. Her lip

trembled. 'It was so very, very beautiful,' she said as the wave carried the mirror away and out of sight, down under the waves forever. 'I loved it *so* much, didn't I? But I couldn't keep it, could I, if it wasn't –'

'Ssh,' said Kate. 'Look.'

Another wave came curling in like a magic green hand reaching out of the sea, opening, spilling out its treasure of shells and pebbles and trailing green weed.

But when it had whispered away again, '*Tillee – ssh – Tillee – ssh . . .*' Matilda saw that the wave had left something else behind too.

The mermaid's mirror!

'I think the sea king bought her a new one,' said Kate. 'Maybe the little mermaid wants you to keep this magic mirror for yourself for ever and ever.'

'Do you think so?' asked Matilda. 'Oh Kate, do you really think so?'

And when Kate nodded firmly, Matilda

threw her cold goosepimply arms around her neck and gave Tilly's big sister the coldest, saltiest, most mermaidy kiss Kate Beany had ever had in her life!

The Jellybear's Picnic

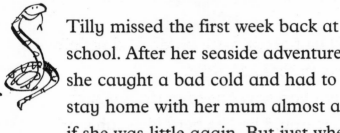

Tilly missed the first week back at school. After her seaside adventures she caught a bad cold and had to stay home with her mum almost as if she was little again. But just when she was beginning to enjoy herself, on the very day she woke up full of wonderful plans to make her own underwater city in the bath (using the dolls' house dolls for mermaids) Tilly's cold was gone. She was well enough to go to school after all.

And as soon as she got to school some exciting news drove the mermaid city out of her mind.

'We're going to the zoo,' said Stephanie. 'We had a letter.'

86

'The zoo!' shouted Tilly. 'How amazing!'

'You didn't get the letter because you were ill,' said Alice.

'We're going *next* week,' said Shazna. 'We're going to see the chimps have their tea.'

'They have it twice a day and people can watch,' said Natalie.

Tilly had never been to the zoo. She hoped it would be like her old Noah's ark, with all the creatures roaming around two by two for all the visitors to stroke, and kind humans with round rosy faces like the wooden Noah family to feed the animals.

But Nathan said it wasn't like that at all. The animals in the zoo were very dangerous, he said. 'That's why they're shut up in cages,' he said. 'So they can't eat the people. That's why the zookeepers push the food in through the bars with long sticks, so the lions and tigers can't grab the keepers in their hooky claws and eat them for dinner as well.'

'I don't believe you,' said Tilly. She thought Nathan was getting mixed up with prisons.

'It's true! It *is true*, silly Tilly,' Nathan shouted. 'Silly Tilly. Silly Tilly,' he sang.

Nathan always got excited about this kind of thing. He started pretending to be the brave zookeeper and Steven rushed around the tables roaring, pretending to be the dangerous lion.

'Back! Back! Get back,' Nathan ordered.

Miss Hinchin had to tell him twice to sit down in his seat.

Tilly didn't think Noah ever shut his animals in cages. Except maybe just the little ones and that was only so they didn't get lost or fall in the water. She hoped Nathan never met her mermaid. He'd think she should be put in a cage too.

I'm not sure if I do like zoos, she said to herself.

When Tilly got home she gave her mum the letter about the school trip.

'The zoo!' said Tilly's mum. 'You've never been to the zoo, Tilly, have you?'

'No,' agreed Tilly. 'They put the animals in cages, don't they?' She was still hoping Nathan might be wrong.

'Yes,' said her mum. 'I'm afraid they do. But I suppose it is nice for children to see all the animals. I always like the monkeys. But their faces look so sad.'

'Do I have to go?' asked Tilly.

'Of course not,' said her mum. 'Don't you want to?'

'I don't know,' said Tilly. 'I *might* do.'

But in the end, because she didn't know how to explain about the mermaid to Miss Hinchin, Tilly decided to go after all. If she didn't, Miss Hinchin would only laugh as usual and say what a wonderful imagination Tilly had.

The night before the zoo trip, Tilly said,

'Do you think the animals know if some of the children don't like the cages?'

'I'm sure they do, Jellybean,' said her dad. 'Look, I've bought you a treat to eat in the bus on your way to the zoo. Not jellybeans, and not jellybabies, but jellybears.'

'Bite the heads off first when you eat them,' advised Sophie. 'That's what I do. Then they don't feel it at all.'

'Tilly's planning something again,' said Tilly's mum, after Tilly had gone to bed.

'How do you know?' said Tilly's dad.

'I can tell. Her eyes get greener and rounder and she keeps going off by herself.'

'She has been mysterious,' agreed Tilly's dad. 'And I heard someone poking around in that old dressing-up box upstairs. Well, I expect we'll find out all about it tomorrow.'

But even so Tilly's dad had a shock when he went into Tilly's room next morning.

Tom was fast asleep as usual. But Tilly had vanished again. And curled up, snoring very faintly under Tilly's quilt with the tiny strawberry pattern on it, was a small furry bear. Tilly's dad could tell it was a girl bear because it was wearing Tilly's nightie.

'How extraordinary,' said Tilly's dad. 'This is just like Goldilocks, only the baby bear is sleeping in the little girl's bed, instead of the other way round!'

Just then the little bear woke up and started rubbing her eyes with her furry paws. For a moment she looked a bit

surprised to see them sticking out of the sleeves of her nightie, as if maybe she hadn't had paws for very long.

'Is it morning already?' she asked.

'It is,' said Tilly's dad. 'Have you got a name, little bear?'

'Yes, Jellybear,' said the little bear, yawning. 'And I'd like blackberry jelly and peanut butter sandwiches in my lunchbox today, please, same as Tilly.'

The children were surprised when Jellybear turned up at school wearing Tilly's new blue jacket and carrying Tilly's lunchbox. The little bear was also carrying a large carrier bag and she wouldn't tell anyone what she'd got in it. Not even Stephanie.

Everyone wanted to sit next to Jellybear on the coach so they could stroke her fur, and hold her paw, but Miss Hinchin said Jellybear had to sit next to *her*. 'Taking a bear to the zoo is the silliest thing I ever heard of,' she said crossly. 'Anyway, you'll get far too hot inside all that fur.'

'I won't,' Jellybear told her. 'You'll see.'

Jellybear seemed perfectly happy sitting on the coach, looking out of the window as they rushed along the motorway. She sang quietly to herself in a growly little voice. 'Today's the day the Jellybear has her pic – nic.'

She sang the song when they got off the coach. And when they all went through the turnstile into the zoo.

At first Miss Hinchin was so cross that she kept a fierce hold of Jellybear's paw as they walked along. But after a while she noticed people smiling at them. After a little while longer, Miss Hinchin found she was beginning to smile herself. It wasn't as if Jellybear was behaving badly. In fact she was behaving much better than most of the other children.

'If you promise to be a good bear, Tilly,'

said Miss Hinchin, feeling rather proud of herself, 'you can hold Stephanie's hand now, instead.'

'My name's Jellybear,' the little bear reminded her politely. 'Thank you, Miss Hinchin.'

Jellybear scampered off right away, clutching her carrier bag and humming her Jellybear song.

There was lots to see at the zoo. By lunchtime they still hadn't seen it all. They ate their sandwiches beside the big pool, watching the sea lions playing in the water.

After lunch they went to the reptile house because Miss Hinchin knew it would be warm in there and the children were getting rather chilly. Except Jellybear, of course, who was as warm as toast in her fur coat. Miss Hinchin began to wish she was wearing one too.

No one liked the snakes and lizards much. Pritesh said the smell made him feel sick.

'I want to see the chimps,' said Natalie. 'I want to see them drink their tea out of real cups like they do on the telly.'

Miss Hinchin sighed. 'I think it's time everyone went to the toilet again,' she said.

It took Jellybear a long time to come out of the Ladies. Miss Hinchin supposed she was having trouble with her fur.

'Anyone seen Jellybear?' she called. 'Does she need any help?'

Shazna shook her head. 'She's not here, Miss. She ran off when you were washing your hands.'

'Oh, no,' moaned Miss Hinchin. 'Why didn't one of you say?'

'She said she'd bite us if we did,'

explained Alice.

'This is dreadful,' said Miss Hinchin. 'The rest of you can go with Steven's mum and wait for the chimps' tea party to begin, and I'll go and look for Jelly, er Tilly . . .'

But although Miss Hinchin searched everywhere she could think of she couldn't find Jellybear at all. Supposing Jellybear had fallen in the sea lions' pool. Supposing she had been eaten by a great big – Don't panic, said Miss Hinchin to herself. She must be here somewhere. I'll just keep very calm and in a minute I'm sure to find her.

Perhaps Miss Hinchin should have asked someone to help her straight away. But she went hot and cold every time she even thought about having to explain to anyone that she had brought a little girl in a bear suit on a school trip to the zoo – and then *lost* her. It sounded so silly! But she had to do it in the end. Poor Miss Hinchin.

Soon a little crowd had formed around Miss Hinchin. A teenage boy whooshed up on his skateboard and took off his headphones so that he could listen better to what was going on.

'Hey,' he interrupted. 'Are you looking for that funny little girl in the bear suit?'

'Yes,' said Miss Hinchin. 'Have you seen her? Where was she? Was she all right?'

'She looked fine to me,' said the boy. 'She was having a tea party all by herself out of a doll's tea set. Everyone was enjoying watching her while they were waiting for the chimps to start theirs. She was better than the chimps really. She was better than the telly. She was telling everyone how much animals hate being shut up in –'

'Take me to her *now*,' interrupted Miss Hinchin rudely.

'Oh, right, I get you. "Follow that bear!"' said the boy, grinning, and off he

 whooshed with Miss Hinchin racing after him. By the time they arrived Jellybear was already packing her tea party away.

Everyone was clapping and looking rather sorry that it was all over, so the crowd cheered as the boy skateboarded up with Miss Hinchin tearing along behind him, very pink in the face by now, and extremely angry.

'That's quite enough of this nonsense, Tilly Beany. You've got to come home with me at once,' ordered Miss Hinchin, holding out her hand.

But before she put her paw into her teacher's hand, Jellybear put her little china teapot carefully back into her carrier bag, which seemed fuller than Miss Hinchin remembered. She didn't make a fuss at all and she didn't look even slightly ashamed, considering how naughty she'd been, Miss Hinchin thought. In fact, she seemed a little bit pleased with herself.

'She's right, you know,' an old lady was saying. 'I just never thought about it. I wouldn't want a herd of little kids staring at me while I was eating my beans on toast.'

'It isn't nice,' whispered a little boy to Miss Hinchin. 'It isn't kind to laugh at the chimps and make them sit on chairs like

people. They've got feelings just like us. We wouldn't like it. That's what the Jellybear said. She said chimps like messing about in the jungle, and swinging in the trees. Can I have the Jellybear's autograph?'

Miss Hinchin didn't answer. She only swooped down like a big angry bird for just long enough to pick up Tilly's lunchbox and drop it into her own large teacher's bag, then she began to head back to the coach as fast as she could. This was so very fast indeed that the other children in Tilly's class and the mums who had come along to help out, had to run after her too, to keep up. And Miss Hinchin had such tight hold of Jellybear's paw that the poor little bear was gasping as she was towed along at her teacher's side, her other paw dragged almost down to the ground by the strangely full carrier bag.

Even though Jellybear's little back paws were twinkling along so fast they hardly touched the ground, she still kept trying to say something. But Miss Hinchin was much too angry to listen to her. 'We've had quite enough from *you*,' was all Tilly's teacher would say, every time Jellybear opened her mouth.

By the time they reached the coach Jellybear was so out of breath she couldn't speak at all. She didn't recover until the coach was rumbling home through the misty, grey afternoon. At last she tugged at Miss Hinchin's coat and said anxiously, 'Miss Hinchin –'

'Don't you dare even try to speak to me for the rest of this trip, Jelly Beany,' snapped Miss Hinchin. She was so tired and cross by now she was a bit mixed up. 'I am very very cross with you. Goodness *knows* what your mother and father will have to say when I tell them.'

'But, Miss Hinchin,' said Jellybear. 'Please – I just want to know, what should

I do with all these?'

Very carefully, so as not to damage anything, the little bear emptied out her carrier bag.

And when she saw what was inside the bag Miss Hinchin's eyes opened very wide. For there were jam doughnuts and cream buns, chocolate bars and sherbet dips, packets of crisps, apples, tangerines . . .

'There's enough for a feast,' said Miss Hinchin in astonishment. 'Wherever did you get those, Je – Tilly?'

'It was for my Jellybear's Picnic,'

explained Jellybear. 'The people gave them to me. I thought it would be rude to leave them behind. I tried and tried to tell you, Miss Hinchin.

Should I throw them away now?'

The other children were crowding up to the front of the coach now, peering over the back of Miss Hinchin's seat, their mouths watering.

'I dropped my sandwiches in the sea lions' pool by mistake, Miss,' said Steven.

'Mine went all squishy,' said Natalie. 'I hate it when my mum puts tomato in them.'

'I'm starving,' said Ben. 'I left my lunch at home by mistake.'

'I was too excited to eat mine,' said Shazna. 'I threw it in the bin.'

Miss Hinchin was worn out. She was hungry, too, now she came to think about it. Like Shazna she'd been too nervous to enjoy her lunch. Suddenly, perhaps because she was so very tired, her lips began to twitch, her eyes began to twinkle in a very un-Miss Hinchinish way, and she started to laugh.

'All right, children,' she said. 'Today I've done two things that I've never ever done before and that I never ever plan to do again. Taken a bear on a school trip to the zoo and *lost* her there –'

'Please, Miss, and you chased a skateboard too, Miss,' interrupted Stephanie gently. 'We didn't know you were such a good runner, Miss.'

'Yes, Stephanie, dear,' said Miss Hinchin who had been hoping everyone had forgotten that. 'Well, we never got to see the chimpanzees' tea party after all, did we, so in case some of you are a little bit disappointed we may as well finish the day with the First and Last Jellybear's Picnic in the world.'

And Miss Hinchin helped herself greedily to the largest, squishiest cream doughnut!

'Yes!' shouted the children. 'Hurray! Hurray for Jellybear and the Jellybear's Picnic!'

But as the children passed buns and

crisps to the back of the coach Jellybear was gazing at Miss Hinchin as if she had never really seen her before.

Miss Hinchin's cheeks were still pink from running. Her eyes were still bright from laughing. And there was a great big blob of cream on her chin. This was a very different Miss Hinchin from the usual one.

Perhaps Miss Hinchin was a tiny bit like Tilly Beany. Perhaps Tilly's teacher was too big inside to be the same person every day too. Jellybear was filled with sympathy. Perhaps Miss Hinchin had to work very hard at being the same person all the time, so as not to muddle all the children.

Suddenly the little bear leaned across and squeezed Miss Hinchin's hand with her sticky furry paw.

'Hurray for you,' she whispered. 'Hurray for taking us to the zoo. I think you are the nicest teacher in the whole world, Miss Hinchin.'

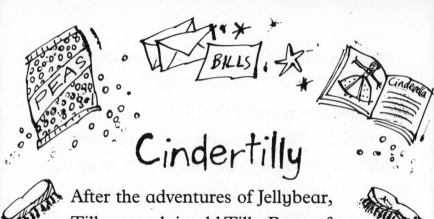

Cindertilly

After the adventures of Jellybear, Tilly was plain old Tilly Beany for a long time. Tilly didn't even go *near* the dressing-up box for weeks and weeks.

'Peace at last,' said Tilly's dad one evening. 'Tilly's finally turning over a new leaf.'

'Hmm,' said Tilly's mum, who wasn't so sure.

But Miss Hinchin was delighted when Tilly's mum and dad went along to the parents' evening. 'Tilly's settling in nicely, now,' she said. 'She just needed a firm hand.'

'Huh,' snorted Tilly's mum, but she changed it into a cough and

106

added politely, 'I'm sure you're right, Miss Hinchin.'

She was relieved that Tilly was behaving herself though, because recently the Beanys had a whole lot of new worries. They came all at once in a big crowd, the way worries always do. Suddenly the whole family was talking about bills and money and how Tom and Tilly needed bedrooms of their own now they were older.

'But we just can't afford a bigger house,' sighed Tilly's dad one weekend, as he added up the same numbers for the third time and still couldn't make it come out right. 'And we never will unless someone comes along and waves a magic wand.' He looked sad and tired. He'd been looking sad and tired all week, thought Tilly.

Tilly was worried. She wanted to help. But she was only five. She knew she couldn't go out to work and earn the money to buy a new house by herself.

'Never mind, Jellybean. This is our own cosy, friendly little house, isn't it?' said Tilly's dad, seeing how serious Tilly was looking. 'We'll manage somehow, won't we?'

'Yes,' agreed Tilly thoughtfully.

Then, next day at school, just before the going-home story, an amazing thing happened. Miss Hinchin gave out the parts in the Christmas play and, because Tilly had been so good, she told Tilly she could be the Christmas tree fairy!

Tilly just beamed happily all through the story, which was *Borka the Goose* again. Fairies. Of course! Tilly had forgotten all about fairies. Everything was going to be all right after all. She couldn't wait to get home and tell everyone.

'That's lovely, Tilly. Well done,' said Tilly's mum when Tilly told her excitedly about the play. But she didn't really understand, Tilly could see, and no one else was even a little bit interested.

Kate was in a bad mood when she got home. She said Sophie had made a mess of their bedroom. Sophie said she hadn't. Kate went stomping upstairs with the hoover to clean it anyway.

Tom didn't listen to Tilly's news either. He was grumpy too. He'd got soaked through coming back from his piano lesson in the rain, and just raced past Tilly dripping and grumbling, looking for a dry towel.

They didn't understand yet, she sighed. But they would. Tilly Beany hugged herself hard. She couldn't wait to see how proud of her they were going to be. Her family didn't think five-year-old girls could make a difference. But they could. Oh, yes they could!

'Have we *got* a fairy's dress in the dressing-up box, Tilly?' asked Sophie, airily knocking the spit out of her clarinet just as if she couldn't hear Kate hoovering angrily upstairs.

Tilly's mum was trying to make supper but the freezer drawer was stuck and she was having trouble getting the peas out.

'No,' said Tilly, puzzled. 'I'm having a real fairy dress with real fairy sparkle stuff on it. Not an old dressing-up one, Sophie. I'm going to be a real fairy.'

But still no one was really listening.

'Mum,' said Tom, coming back in the

kitchen with the towel over his head. 'I need new shoes. My feet got soaking every time I went out today.'

Sophie heard this through her clarinet playing and stopped with a squawk. 'You can't have new shoes, Tom Beany. I need a jacket first. Mum promised me one ages ago.'

'Here, let me help,' said Tilly's dad to Tilly's mum who was still trying to unstick the freezer drawer. He gave it such a hard tug it came out in a rush. Frozen peas flew everywhere like little green hailstones.

At the same moment, upstairs, the hoover gave a coughing sound as if it was trying to swallow something too big for it, then it stopped altogether. The air filled with a smell of burning rubber.

'Mum,' yelled Kate from upstairs. 'The hoover's broken. I think we need a new one.'

Tilly's dad groaned. 'If things go on like this we may have to cancel Christmas,' he said. And Tilly knew he was only half joking.

'Don't worry,' Tilly said softly to her mum and dad, hugging them both, almost bursting with her lovely secret. 'Everything's going to be fine. I know it is.'

'Oh dear,' said Tilly's dad when Tilly had gone to bed. 'What's Tilly up to now? Her eyes have gone very green and round again. Who am I going to find when I go into Tilly's room tomorrow morning? I'm not sure I can stand any more excitement just now.'

But next morning it was only plain old Tilly Beany fast asleep under her strawberry-patterned quilt.

And it was only plain old Tilly Beany who came home again, good as gold. She even dried up the knives and forks after supper without being asked and put them away slowly and carefully in the right parts of the drawer, instead of throwing them in

higgledy-piggledy and dashing off to play
as she usually did.

'You aren't actually turning *into* a good
fairy, are you?' Tilly's dad asked that
evening as Tilly climbed on to his knee to
read her new reading book.

'No, Daddy, I'm only Tilly now. Why?'

'I just thought maybe some magic
sparkle dust was rubbing off that fairy
costume on to you, Tilly,' he teased her. 'Are
you sure you aren't up to something?'

'No, *really* I'm not, Daddy. And I
haven't got my costume yet. But I'm getting
it soon.'

But Tilly's eyes were sparkling just as
if some magic dust *had* got into them.

Next day Nathan's mum brought the
costumes for the play into school at last.

'Here's yours, Tilly,' said Miss Hinchin,
handing her a carrier bag. 'Try them on
over your jeans for now.'

Tilly's heart was beating so loudly she

thought everyone must be able to hear it as she took out the sparkly fairy dress and quickly put it on. There was some more sparkly tinsel for Tilly to wear on her head, too. Stephanie helped her with that. Then Tilly felt around excitedly at the bottom of the carrier bag. But there was nothing there.

'Where's my magic wand?' she said. 'Did it fall out?'

'Sorry, dear?' Miss Hinchin was trying to sort out Ben's mouse costume. The tail was so long and traily the other children kept tripping over it. Natalie had already banged her head once.

'My magic wand. To do my magic with. Did it fall out?' Tilly was beginning to look upset.

'Well, if you really need to have one, perhaps your mum can make it,' suggested Miss Hinchin. She sounded as if she thought Tilly was making a silly fuss about nothing.

'I'll make you one, Tilly,' said Nathan's

mum. 'You're right. Of course a fairy should have a wand. Don't worry. I was in such a hurry to get the other costumes done that I forgot to make your wand but I've got plenty of glitter left over. And I can easily find a piece of wood to make it with.'

'You don't understand,' said Tilly. Her chin was trembling. 'You can't *make* a magic wand out of wood. Not a real wand that does real magic.'

Now Tilly could see how home-made the other costumes looked: Alice's, Shazna's and Ben's. Steven's robot costume was a dustbin bag sprayed silver, with sprayed silver rubber gloves for his hands. She could see where it said "cornflakes" on Steven's big square robot helmet.

But Tilly's Christmas tree fairy's costume was the most home-made costume of all. It didn't even stick out properly the way fairy dresses should. It drooped like a dead moth. Tilly knew she didn't look like

a fairy in it. She looked
like a funny little girl
wearing someone's
old underwear with
Christmas cake
decorations glued
on to it.

Tilly stared down at
the dead-moth skirt,
with her old jeans and
red woolly socks poking out of the bottom.
She looked so terrible she couldn't say a
single word.

But before she could stop them, huge
tears came rolling down her face, splashing
her shoes. Tilly Beany had been going to
put everything right. She'd been going to
magic her mum and dad a big house and
enough money for shoes, jackets and new
hoovers, with plenty left over for lovely
Christmas presents for everyone. But it had
all gone wrong. Tilly Beany wanted to run

away before anyone else realised what a stupid mistake she had made.

Miss Hinchin and Nathan's mum were staring at Tilly now. They were beginning to understand.

'Did you think you'd get a *real* magic wand with your costume, Tilly?' asked Nathan's mum gently.

'Yes,' whispered Tilly. Though she was sniffing back her tears as hard as she could, more kept leaking out from somewhere. She couldn't keep up with them. 'Or how could I do my magic?' she asked them.

Miss Hinchin sighed. 'It's just a play, Tilly dear. It's just pretend. There's no such thing as magic, really, you know.'

'Yes, there is,' shouted Tilly. 'Because I've got a real mermaid's mirror, and I'll find a real magic wand too, so there.'

But she was only shouting so no one could see how unhappy she was. Because if anyone ever guessed how silly she had been,

Tilly Beany knew she would die.

When Tilly's mum came to meet her out of school that afternoon, Tilly didn't say a word. She couldn't tell anyone. And she knew she couldn't be the fairy in the Christmas play any more either and how was she going to explain that? She would have to pretend to have tummy ache, because she couldn't wear that stupid droopy underwear dress. She couldn't wave a dead old stick sprayed with Nathan's mum's glitter-stuff.

Miss Hinchin was right. Only babies believed in fairies and magic wands, thought Tilly. Grown-up people knew there was no such thing. Tilly's dad would get sadder and more worried every day and Christmas was going to be cancelled. And Tilly couldn't do anything to help because she was only five. It was the worst day of Tilly Beany's life.

That night, before Tilly went to bed,

there was a magic show on television but Tilly knew it wasn't real magic but just tricks.

'Abracadabra!' cried a smiling man in a shiny suit. 'That's the magic word, ladies and gentlemen.'

Tilly could see he didn't really believe in magic words. The magician tapped his empty top hat with his wand which was a shiny black stick, not a real wand at all, and a cloud of white birds flew out. Everyone clapped just as if he'd done some real magic and suddenly Tilly burst into noisy tears.

'What's the matter, what are the tears for, Jellybean?' asked Tilly's dad. He was trying to mend the hoover and watch television at the same time.

'Because I hate that Abracadabra man,' Tilly wept. 'He's a liar, anyway. I want to go to bed,' she wailed. 'I want Kate to read me a story.'

Kate put down her homework and hugged Tilly as hard as she could. 'Don't cry, Tilly. Of course I'll read to you.'

Tilly was only sniffing by the time she climbed into bed, but when her sister took the big fairytale book down from the shelf she began crying angrily all over again.

'I don't *want* a magic story,' Tilly howled. 'There isn't any magic any more. Magic isn't true.'

'Yes it is,' said Kate. 'Maybe not just the same as the magic in fairy stories. But magic things happen, all the same. What about those boring little hyacinth bulbs you planted with Mum? How did they turn themselves into green leaves? Isn't that magic? How do you know those dry dull little things weren't wishing and dreaming they might turn into leaves and flowers and one day – whoosh! Their dream came true.'

Tilly stopped crying. 'Hyacinths can't dream, silly,' she said in a wobbly voice. 'Hyacinths can't wish.'

'How do you know?' asked Kate. 'How do you know what secrets they have tucked away inside them? How do you know what secrets are tucked away inside *you*?'

Tilly gave an extra big sniff, but she was listening carefully now. She was remembering how big and magic it sometimes felt to be Tilly Beany, however small and ordinary she might look in the mirror. She was remembering that sometimes she was big enough to have storms and rainbows inside.

'Take Cinderella,' Kate went on, opening the big fairytale book. 'She thought she'd got to stay in that great big house doing all the cleaning by herself and having to wait on the mean old ugly sisters hand and foot.

121

She thought every day was going to be the same: getting up at six to scrub the front step, nothing but dirty rags to wear and horrible dried bread to eat. The ugly sisters told Cinderella that no one would *ever* love her, but inside her dirty old rags Cinderella never stopped wishing and dreaming. Even when she was cleaning the nasty, greasy stove she would sing to herself a soft little wishing, dreaming song and one day, when Cinderella was all alone in the house, there was a loud knock at the . . .'

Kate stopped. 'I forgot. You don't want to hear any more stories about magic, do you, Tilly?' she said, starting to close the book again.

'You can read it, Kate,' said Tilly, quickly. 'If you like.'

And she wriggled down under her quilt, as close to her big sister Kate as she could get. The longer Tilly listened to the story, the rounder and greener her eyes became in the lamplight. And she didn't get sleepier while Kate was reading. She only closed her eyes so she could listen to the story better. Behind her eyelids Tilly Beany was growing more wide awake every minute.

At last Kate closed the book, switched off the lamp and tiptoed away.

Tilly sat up. For a while she sat cosily in her bed, staring around at the friendly darkness of her bedroom, humming a soft wishing, dreaming song to herself. After another minute she switched her lamp back on. Then she got out of bed and pattered across the landing to the boxroom . . .

'Tilly's not in her bed,' shouted Tilly's dad the next morning. 'Where on earth has she gone?'

'She can't have vanished,' Tilly's mum yelled from the bathroom through a mouthful of toothpaste. 'I expect she's gone downstairs to get herself some cereal.'

'But Tilly's always fast asleep in the mornings,' said Tilly's dad to himself. 'Curled up tight like a sleepy little dormouse. And she's taken her night things off but she hasn't put her school clothes on.'

'Are you looking for Tilly, Dad?' asked Tom, coming upstairs, grinning all over his face. 'She's been up for *hours*. She's outside the front door scrubbing the step for some reason. I didn't know people did that any more. Well, it's not Tilly, exactly, it's a rather dirty ragged little girl who says she's called –'

'Oh, no,' groaned Tilly's dad. 'Don't tell me – Kate!' he roared. 'What did you read to Tilly last night?'

'Cinderella,' came a sleepy mumble

124

from Kate and Sophie's room.

'Well, thank you, Kate Beany,' said Tilly's dad. 'Now I've got to eat breakfast with poor ragged little – *Cindertilly.*'

He dashed downstairs still wearing his pyjamas. The front door stood open, letting in a great deal of cold air but Cindertilly was nowhere to be seen. There was just a huge puddle slowly spreading itself across a very clean doorstep.

A splashy criss-cross trail of footprints on the hall carpet showed where Cindertilly had carried her big bucket of soapy water in and out of the kitchen all by herself.

Tilly's dad followed the footprints to where a ragged, dirty, barefoot little girl with tangled hair was hacking at a lump of stale bread with a very large knife, singing softly to herself.

'Cindertilly?' said Tilly's dad, turning the little girl to face him. Cindertilly jumped with surprise. She was rather damp as if some of her had got washed at the same time as the step.

'I've cleaned the step, Father,' said Cindertilly quickly. 'And I did the washing-up Sophie left last night. I haven't cleaned the cooker yet but I promise I'll do it before I go to school.'

'And what are you planning to do with the stale bread?'

'I'm making my lunch,' explained Cindertilly.

'But Tilly likes blackberry jelly sandwiches and bananas and cherry yoghurt.' Tilly's dad was beginning to shiver. His pyjamas were quite thin. Cindertilly must have left the front door open for a long time.

'My stepmother only lets me eat dried crusts,' said the ragged girl in a sad voice.

'And I don't suppose she gives you any shoes, either,' shivered Tilly's dad. 'Or any warm clothes.' He wondered why Cindertilly wasn't shivering too. Perhaps doing so much cleaning warmed her up.

'No, she doesn't. I'm very very poor and ragged, aren't I? But I know it's not *your* fault, Father.' Cindertilly yawned. 'Sorry,' she said, 'I had to get up ever so early to scrub the step. In a minute I've got to go and make Sophie look beautiful, though it will be very hard . . .' She yawned again.

'Cindertilly, didn't you get any sleep at all?' asked Tilly's dad.

'Not really. I wasn't sure when six o'clock was so I stayed awake in case I missed hearing the downstairs clock strike.'

Tilly's dad sighed. He seemed to be thinking hard. Suddenly he said, 'Just a minute, Cindertilly, don't cut yourself another *single* dry crust till I get back,' and went dashing back upstairs again.

Cindertilly could hear voices murmuring upstairs as she got the scouring pad and started work on the dirty cooker. Once she thought she heard Tilly's dad say, 'Really out of hand,' and, 'Needs someone who understands,' and she might have heard Tilly's mum say, 'Well, all right, I'll ring her, but I can't think why she should help us.'

Then, Tilly's dad came dashing back downstairs. He was still fastening his shirt buttons. Cindertilly was surprised to see that he was looking very cross and not like Tilly's dad at all.

'Cindertilly,' he said, 'you can't go to school today.'

Cindertilly was even more surprised to hear this. 'But I've nearly cleaned the cooker. Why can't I go?'

'Because there's still the whole house to clean from top to bottom,' he said in a fierce voice. 'You haven't been working *nearly* hard enough. And tonight your stepmother is giving a grand party – though of course *you* won't be able to come to it, Cindertilly,' he added, rather out of breath, 'so we need everything to be as clean and bright as a new pin.'

He said the last bit in a specially loud voice at just the same time as Tilly's mum started talking to someone on the phone in the hall.

'Oh,' said Cindertilly. She rubbed harder at a big black mark on the cooker and hummed a bit more of her wishing, dreaming tune but her voice wobbled. She looked a bit frightened, too.

'Will I have to cook all the food for the party as well?' she asked bravely.

'No,' said Tilly's dad in his new rough,

cross voice. 'The cook will do that.'

'Oh,' said Cindertilly.

Cindertilly didn't know what to think. Actually she wasn't sure if she was Cindertilly any more. She thought perhaps she wasn't. She thought she might have turned into plain old Tilly Beany again, but she wasn't sure anyone in her family would believe her now. They might make her stay Cindertilly for ever and ever. At this thought, she felt so frightened and unhappy she couldn't even cry.

Sophie had left her big red cardigan in the kitchen for Cindertilly to mend when she'd finished the cleaning. After looking at it longingly for a minute, Tilly put it on over her rags. It was nice to feel warm again. She thought she might put Tilly's own cosy tiger's feet slippers on her bare feet too.

Tilly was very lonely. Tom, Kate and Sophie were at school. Tilly's dad had gone off to work. Her mum was upstairs. Tilly's mum said she had a headache and needed some peace and quiet. So why had she been talking on the phone so early in the morning? And who had she been talking to?

Tilly sat down, and because she didn't know even where to begin cleaning the whole house by herself, especially now the hoover was broken, she rested her tired head for a little while on the kitchen table, still humming bravely to herself. Perhaps she went to sleep for just a minute because she jumped when she thought she heard the Beanys' car pull up outside. But then the car went away again and no one turned a key in the lock and no one called out, 'I'm home,' and no one came in the kitchen to put the kettle on.

Tilly was still all by herself.

But what was that?

She could hear footsteps, slow, soft footsteps. And then a soft knock-knocking on the door. Not the front door, but the back door. And a soft, rather old-sounding voice calling, 'Tilly, Tilly Beany. Won't you let me in?'

And when Tilly went to the door and opened it there was a tiny old lady standing outside, a very elegant old lady with snowy white hair, dressed beautifully in black from head to toe and carrying an enormous black bag.

'Are you my fairy godmother?' she asked, feeling trembly. It was scary, coming face to face with real magic at last.

'Of course,' said the old lady cheerfully. 'Who did you think it was? Aren't you going to let me in?'

Abracadabra!

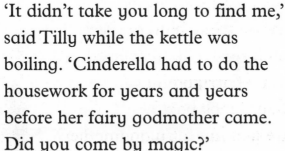

'It didn't take you long to find me,' said Tilly while the kettle was boiling. 'Cinderella had to do the housework for years and years before her fairy godmother came. Did you come by magic?'

'No, dear,' said the old lady. 'Your father fetched me in the car though I'm afraid it made him rather late for work. But I *have* brought you a dress almost beautiful enough for Cinderella.'

She sat down comfortably at the kitchen table and began to rummage through her black bag. 'It might be rather too big. But I'm sure your mum or one of your clever sisters could shorten the straps for you.'

Shorten the straps! That didn't sound very magic, thought Tilly. Surely fairy godmothers simply waved their wands with a whisk and a frisk and the dress fitted perfectly, first time?

But just then the old lady pulled out a dress so beautiful that Tilly gasped.

It was as white and sparkling as a snowflake. It didn't droop like a dead moth, or flop like anyone's old underwear, but stuck out properly all around itself just the way it should, like a ballerina's tutu.

A real fairy's dress.

'Try it on, if you like it, Tilly, dear,' said the old lady. 'I'll make the tea.'

The fairy godmother stood up, walked across the kitchen and began looking in the cupboards for cups and saucers. Even though she was so old she walked with a very straight back, thought Tilly, holding her head as proudly as a queen. In fact she didn't really seem to *walk* at all. She seemed to glide.

Tilly looked quickly at the old lady's shoes to make quite sure they were still touching the ground, not hovering in the air. You never knew with fairy godmothers. But the shoes just went tiptapping normally across the kitchen tiles exactly like an ordinary person's shoes.

They weren't ordinary, though. They were black, like the rest of the old lady's clothes, and made out of very soft leather, more like gloves than shoes, with straps that fastened at the side with a tiny black button. And although the shoes had a pointy look they were just a little bit blunt at the toes. Like a witch's shoes.

And Tilly Beany knew she had seen those shoes before.

Tilly didn't put on the fairy dress. She just stood and stared. Who could this peculiar, beautifully-dressed old lady be and why had she come to see Tilly? Something very strange was going on.

Tilly's eyes stopped being round and green. They went narrow and green instead, the way they did when she was thinking especially hard.

'Are you the lady my mum phoned up?' Tilly asked. 'Did *she* ask you to come and see me?'

The old lady calmly put two tea bags in the pot and poured in the boiling water. She seemed at home in the Beanys' kitchen. 'That's right, dear,' she said. 'Do you like sugar in your tea?'

'I don't like tea at all,' said Tilly rudely. 'You *aren't* a fairy godmother, are you? Who are you really? Why did my mum and dad ask you to come?'

'Well,' said the old lady, sitting down

and making herself comfortable again, 'you won't remember me, Tilly, but I remember you perfectly. Once upon a time I used to be a dancing teacher, you know. I was a very good one too. I taught your big sister Kate when she was younger.'

Tilly remembered the Jellybear costume. Kate had worn it first when she was the baby bear in a ballet about Goldilocks. All at once Tilly remembered something else.

She remembered where she had seen those witchy shoes before.

They weren't witch's shoes at all. They were dance shoes!

Tilly had been very small, still small enough to ride in the Beanys' old pushchair, and her mum had taken her to fetch Kate from her ballet class. Tilly had loved every minute of it. She still remembered a smell of lavender and there had been an old lady wearing a long dress that was lavender, too, but her mum said it wasn't the dress which smelled but the polish on the shiny floor.

The old lady was calling out, 'One and two and three and four!' in a stern, singsong voice. Dozens of little girls in pink ballet shoes stretched up their arms in front of the big mirrors just like real ballet dancers, and a pair of witchy black shoes went tiptapping across the polished wooden floor. Of course!

'You're Miss Violet Gladwell,' she said.

The old lady smiled. 'The Gladwell School of Dance,' she said. 'But many years before I opened that school, Tilly, I used to be an actress.'

'On telly?' said Tilly, her eyes round and

green again.

'No, in the theatre, dear,' corrected Miss Gladwell.

'I went to see a pantomime last Christmas,' said Tilly, remembering. 'That was at the theatre too.'

'But long before I was an actress, Tilly,' the old lady went on, pouring herself out a cup of tea and adding two lumps of sugar, 'I was a little girl very like you. I pretended I was different people all the time. I was always dressing up as someone else. I loved practising different expressions in front of the mirror. I loved to talk in different voices. I thought everyone else was so *dull*. How could they stand being just the same boring person all the time when there were so many other wonderful people to be!'

Tilly stared and stared. 'That's just like me!' she said. She couldn't believe it. On the outside Violet Gladwell was a tiny old lady with wrinkles and white hair, but inside she was a person who knew exactly how it felt to be a little girl who loved dressing-up and pretending to be someone else, more than anything else in the world.

'I thought it might be,' said Miss Gladwell, sipping her tea.

'Maybe I'll be an actress when I grow up too,' said Tilly, beaming. She was feeling much better now Miss Gladwell was here.

'Maybe you will,' said Miss Gladwell, setting down her cup rather sternly in its saucer. 'And maybe not. The thing is, what are we going to do with you now?'

'*Do* with me?' Tilly felt scared again. She had just decided Miss Gladwell was her friend but friends weren't supposed to be fierce.

'Yes. Look at you! You haven't been to sleep all night. Your clothes are soaking wet. Your face is dirty. Your hair is all sticking out like a hedgehog's prickles and here you are, a great big girl of five, mooching around the kitchen at home when you ought to be at school learning how to read and write.'

Tilly thought Miss Gladwell was very unfair.

'My daddy *told* me to stay at home,' she shouted at Miss Gladwell, feeling very sorry for herself. 'Do you *know* what he did? He told me to stay home and clean the *whole* house from top to bottom.'

'Of course he did,' said Miss Gladwell. 'The poor man was at his wit's end. He knew things had got completely out of hand.'

Tilly went quiet. That was what her dad had said to her mum this morning, upstairs while Cindertilly was pretending not to listen. Her dad had been very worried lately. And though Tilly had only wanted to help she had made him more worried than ever, because now he had Tilly to worry about as well as bills and houses that were too small. Tilly wondered if even Miss Gladwell would understand about being Cindertilly singing her wishing and dreaming song, just so the fairy godmother would come and wave her magic wand and make a happy ending for everyone, the way she did in Cinderella.

'So,' Miss Gladwell went on briskly, 'that's why your mother and father asked me to come and sort you out.'

Sort her out! Worse and worse. What would fierce Miss Gladwell do to her? Miss Gladwell had very bright blue eyes. At this moment they were looking so hard at Tilly she was sure the old lady could see through her.

Tilly didn't feel big inside any more. She was shrinking. She was getting smaller every minute.

'So what are you going to do to me?' she said in a little voice to match the new shrinking Tilly.

'Why don't you tell me what you've been doing to yourself, first?' asked the old lady. She was poking around in the big black bag.

'Well, I was a Native American princess called Windstar,' said Tilly, 'and I was an office lady with my own special office called Witchworks and then I was Titch the witch, too, but I fell asleep in the jelly. It was green.'

Miss Gladwell was still shrinking Tilly with her fierce blue eyes. Tilly could hardly find any voice at all now.

'And I was Matilda Seaflower. I had to be a mermaid, because I wanted to give the mirror back,' she explained in a little voice as

thin as a thread. 'And then I went to the zoo but it wasn't nice of them to make the chimps have tea parties so I was a bear and I was called Jellybear and I had my own picnic and all the people gave me things to eat and we ate them on the coach going home. Miss Hinchin took the biggest cream cake. She got it on her chin. And then I was only Tilly Beany for ages but Nathan's mum didn't make me a fairy wand. It wasn't ready and it was only going to be a stick anyway, not a real wand, and the dress was stupid, with cake decorations stuck on it, so then I was Cindertilly because I wanted to –'

Tilly's voice faded away altogether because of the expression on Miss Gladwell's face.

'Hmm,' said Miss Gladwell.

Tilly didn't say anything. She just waited. She was terrified. She wished her mum would come into the kitchen and send fierce Miss Gladwell home again. But her mum was angry with Tilly too. Everyone thought life with Tilly had got 'out of hand', which meant she was so difficult nobody knew what to do with her any more.

Probably nobody loved her any more either.

'Right,' said Miss Gladwell crisply after a long and dreadful silence. 'I've made up my mind.'

'Oh,' squeaked Tilly, squeezing both hands together very hard in case she started to cry.

Miss Gladwell stood up. She looked more like a queen than ever and her blunt-pointy shoes looked witchy again. Was she going to put a spell on Tilly after all?

Tilly stood up, too, on wobbly jelly legs that didn't feel as if they would hold her up for long if things got any worse than this. She shut her eyes tight and whimpered. She didn't want to see what this terrible old lady was going to do.

'Ask your mother to bring you round to my house on Wednesday at tea time,' said Miss Gladwell.

Tilly's eyes flew open.

'Tea time?' repeated Tilly Beany.

'That's right,' said Miss Gladwell. She was putting her gloves back on. 'Every Wednesday from now on, at four-thirty exactly.'

Then, seeing how frightened Tilly looked, she burst out laughing. 'For tea, you silly goose,' she explained. 'What did you *think* I meant?'

'I didn't know,' said Tilly, giving a big sigh of relief, though her legs were still shaking. They hadn't understood the news yet, she thought. Nor had Tilly, quite.

'Look, Tilly, I'm too old to be an actress or a dancer any more. And I'm even too old to be a dancing teacher now. But my life is so dull these days. I miss the excitement. I miss the children and the music and the costumes.

And I'm terribly bored with having to
pretend to be the same ordinary little old
lady every day, when there are so many
different people inside me and I haven't
used up *half* of them yet! So having a friend
like you to visit me for tea once a week
would really cheer me up.'

'You mean –' Tilly's eyes were sparkling
again. She was beginning to understand.

'Of course! You didn't think it was going
to be an ordinary tea party, did you? I
thought this week we might have a pirates'
party –'

'With rum?' said Tilly quickly. 'With rum
and treasure and a stolen map with a skull
on it?'

'Of course,' said Miss Gladwell. 'What
else would you have at a piratical party?
But before we have our tea party, you have
to promise me something, Tilly.'

'Yes, yes – what?' said Tilly, who had
stopped listening properly. She was too

excited about going to tea with Miss Gladwell. Just wait until she told everyone. They would be so jealous!

'Promise me,' said Miss Gladwell, putting two gloved fingers under Tilly's chin and looking right into her round green eyes so she *had* to listen, 'that unless you are playing by yourself or with friends, or you are coming to have tea with me, you will be plain Tilly Beany *all* the rest of the time.'

Tilly looked down at her toes and didn't say a word.

'Just think how confusing it would be,' Miss Gladwell went on, sternly, 'if actors and actresses went on playing their parts even when they weren't on television or in the theatre? Imagine meeting witches and dragons in the supermarket and kings and queens on the buses!'

Tilly knew Miss Gladwell was right but she still felt sad about making the promise.

'Of course,' said the old lady (she was

getting ready to
leave now and
walking towards
the front
door), 'it's up
to you to make
Tilly Beany as
exciting and special
a person as you
possibly can.'

Miss Gladwell was smiling. It was rather
a naughty smile.

'Yes,' said Tilly slowly. 'It is. Thank you.
Oh, Miss Gladwell, you've forgotten your
bag – and the dress.'

'You can borrow the dress, dear, until
the school play is over. And there are some
pirate clothes in there. For our pirate tea,
you know.'

'Ooh,' said Tilly. 'You fibber! You *knew*
you were going to ask me for tea the
whole time!'

Miss Gladwell laughed. 'I *am* an actress, remember. Now *you* should go and wash your face and comb your hair, Tilly Beany,' she said as she opened the front door. 'I look forward to seeing you on Wednesday at four-thirty sharp. Try to be good until then.'

Tilly went back into the kitchen. She thought it would be better not to put the fairy dress on until she had washed herself properly all over, but she couldn't resist peering into Miss Gladwell's big black bag to see what else was inside it.

And then she said, 'Ooh,' and then she said, 'Ooh,' again, because she just didn't know what else to say.

Wrapped up in a soft, magicky-looking piece of red velvet was a fairy wand!

Slender as the stalk of a flower, silver as a star,

with a real star perched on the top as if it had just fallen down out of the sky. And Tilly knew this wand was magic through and through.

It wouldn't magic the Beanys a new house or a pair of shoes for Tom but now she could be the Christmas tree fairy in the school play after all. The best fairy they'd ever had. And she had a friend. A special new friend who knew how it felt to be little on the outside and full of storms and rainbows inside. And Tilly was going to go on wishing and dreaming. Because you never *knew* when the magic was going to turn up.

'*Abracadabra*,' she whispered.

'Abracadabra!' Tilly Beany repeated out loud.

And the magic word sparkled into the air filling the Beanys' kitchen with happiness.

Rainbows
Everywhere

Tilly did go to tea with Miss Gladwell on Wednesday at four-thirty sharp. She went to tea every Wednesday after that.

Sometimes the little girl and the old lady decided who they were going to be in advance. But sometimes they liked to surprise each other, and on those Wednesdays Tilly never knew who was going to open the front door of Miss Violet Gladwell's house and Miss Gladwell never knew *who* she was going to find waiting on her doorstep! Sometimes they surprised each other so much they both laughed and laughed.

'You're like me,' Tilly told the old lady after one of their Wednesday teas. She was squinting through a clever glass ball that hung in Miss Gladwell's window. When Tilly swirled it, tiny rainbows chased each other round the walls making her feel happy and dizzy all at the same time.

'You're quite little on the outside but you've got storms and rainbows inside too.' Then she laughed. 'But it's much nicer now there's two of us. When we're together the rainbows aren't just inside. They're everywhere!'

The Christmas play was a great success. Miss Gladwell came

along with Tilly's mum and dad to watch Tilly playing the part of the Christmas tree fairy. She enjoyed herself so much she asked Miss Hinchin if she could help Nathan's mum with the costumes next time and Miss Hinchin said she could.

And Tilly Beany? Did she keep her promise to Miss Gladwell? Was she being good all this time? Well, of course she was. But Miss Gladwell *had* told her Tilly should make Tilly Beany as exciting and special a person as she possibly could and one day . . .

But that's another story.